LAZY LION

Also by Mwenye Hadithi and Adrienne Kennaway:

Crafty Chameleon
Greedy Zebra
Hot Hippo
Tricky Tortoise

First U.S. Edition

First published in Great Britain in 1990 by Hodder and Stoughton Children's Books, Mill Road, Dunton Green, Sevenoaks, Kent TN13 2YA

ISBN 0-316-33725-0

Library of Congress Catalog Card Number 90-52568

Library of Congress Cataloging-in-Publication information is available.

10 9 8 7 6 5 4 3 2 1

Printed in Belgium

LAZY LION

by **Mwenye Hadithi**

Illustrated by **Adrienne Kennaway**

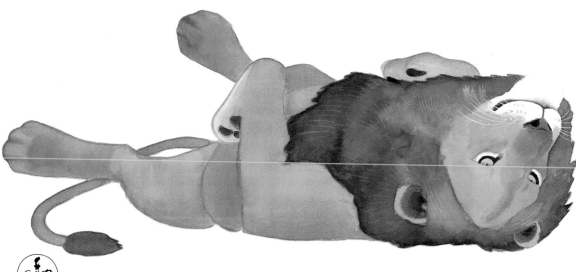

Little, Brown and Company
Boston Toronto London

When the first clouds appeared above the hot African plains, Lazy Lion roared, "The Big Rain is coming. I will need a roof to keep me dry. And since I am the King of the Beasts, I will order a fine house to be built."

So he went to the White Ants.
   "Build me a house," he ordered. "A big house!"
   The White Ants built a palace of towers and
turrets and chimneys and spires.

But Lazy Lion was too big to fit through the door.
"I won't live in the earth," said Lion crossly.

So he went to the Weaver Birds.

"Build me a house," he ordered. "A big house!"

The Weaver Birds built a nest of grasses and palm-leaves and soft fluffy seeds, and it hung from the branch of a thorn tree. But Lazy Lion was too heavy to reach the door.

"I won't live up a tree," said Lion crossly.

So he went to the Aardvarks.

"Build me a house," he ordered. "A big house!"

The Aardvarks dug a huge hole with many rooms and caverns and tunnels and caves. But it was damp and so dark that Lion couldn't see anything.

"I won't live underground," said Lion crossly.

So he went to Honey Badger.

"Build me a house," he ordered. "A big house!"

Honey Badger found a hollow tree stump
and ate all the bees and honeycomb inside it,
and cleaned it as clean as clean, and Lion
climbed inside.

But his head stuck out of the hole in the top, and his tail stuck out of the hole at the bottom.

"I won't live in a tree stump," said Lion crossly.

So he went to Crocodile.

"Build me a house," he ordered. "A big house!"

Crocodile found a cave in the river-bank and swept it with his tail, and Lion walked in and went to sleep. But in the night the cave filled up with water from the river.

"I won't live in the water," said Lion crossly.

By now Lazy Lion was very, very angry, and the sky was absolutely full of big black clouds. So Lion called all the animals together.

"You must ALL build me a house," he ordered. "A VERY, VERY BIG . . ."

But just as he said the words "VERY, VERY BIG," there was a flash of lightning in the sky, and a rumbling of thunder, and suddenly the Big Rain poured down everywhere.

The Aardvarks rushed underground.
Honey Badger trundled off to his tree stump,
and Crocodile waddled into his cave.

The White Ants marched off down their hole.
The Weaver Birds flapped to their nest.

And they all watched Lion sitting in the rain in the middle of the African plain.

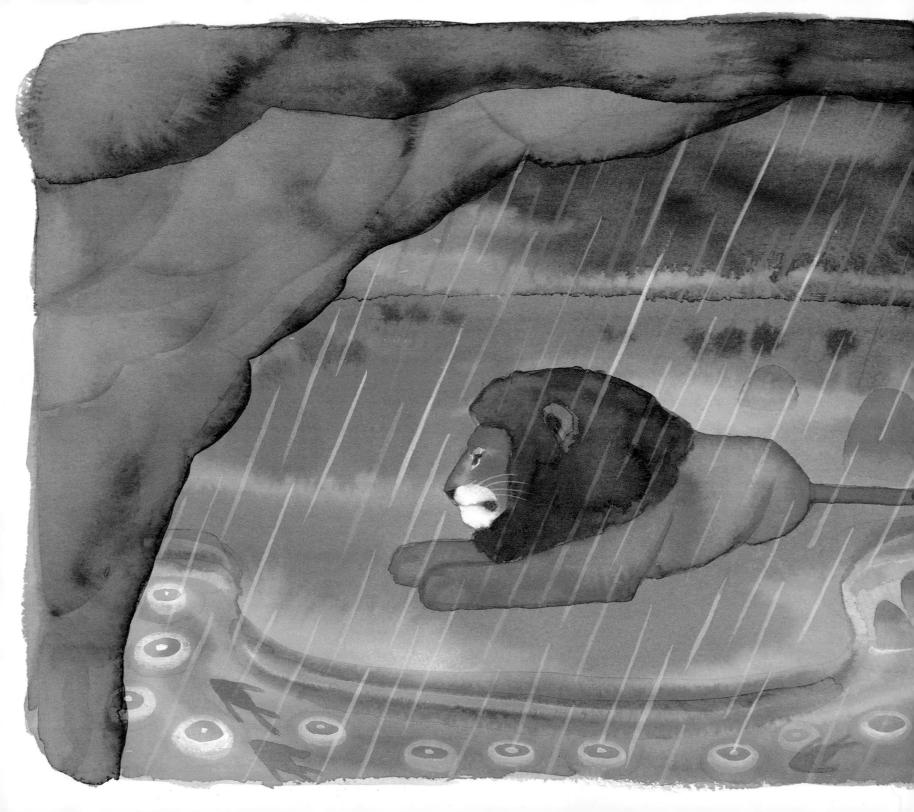

"He is so very difficult to please," said Crocodile, snik-snakking his teeth. And he cried a few tears. Not real ones. Just little crocodile ones.

And to this day, Lion has not found a house to live in.
So he just wanders the African plain. On sunny days
and cloudy days. And even in the Big Rains.